Dear mouse friends,
Welcome to the world of

Geronimo Stilton

THE RODENT'S GAZETTE
EDITORIAL STAFF

Geronimo Stilton
A learned and brainy
mouse; editor of
The Rodent's Gazette

Thea Stilton
Geronimo's sister and
special correspondent at
The Rodent's Gazette

Trap Stilton
An awful joker;
Geronimo's cousin and
owner of the store
Cheap Junk for Less

Benjamin Stilton
A sweet and loving
nine-year-old mouse;
Geronimo's favorite
nephew

Geronimo Stilton

DOWN AND OUT
DOWN UNDER

Scholastic Inc.

New York   Toronto   London   Auckland   Sydney

Mexico City   New Delhi   Hong Kong   Buenos Aires

ISBN 978-0-439-84120-7

Based on an original idea by Elisabetta Dami.

www.geronimostilton.com

Published by Scholastic Inc., 557 Broadway, New York, NY 10012. SCHOLASTIC and associated logos are trademarks and/or registered trademarks of Scholastic Inc.

Stilton is the name of a famous English cheese. It is a registered trademark of the Stilton Cheese Makers' Association. For more information, go to www.stiltoncheese.com

Text by Geronimo Stilton
Original title *È arrivata Patty Spring*
Cover by Silvia Bigolin
Illustrations by Silvia Bigolin
Graphics by Merenguita Gingermouse and Tiziano Finessi

Special thanks to Kathryn Cristaldi
Translated by Lidia Morson Tramontozzi
Interior design by Kay Petronio

15 14 13   11 12 13 14 15 16/0

Printed in the U.S.A.   40
First printing, March 2007

This book is dedicated to all
of my fabumouse friends who
care about the environment!

IT ALL BEGAN WITH A PHONE CALL

I'll admit it. I'm a bit of a 'fraidy mouse. But does that stop me from loving **adventure**? No way! This rodent is up for anything. Well, maybe not anything. I get sick on planes, boats, and when I walk too fast. Still, my last adventure was SUPER-EXCITING.

It all began with a phone **call**. I was at my office when . . . Oops, I almost forgot to introduce myself! My name is Stilton, *Geronimo Stilton*. I am the publisher of the most famouse

Hello?!

newspaper on Mouse Island, *The Rodent's Gazette.*

Anyway, that day the phone rang.

"Hello, Stilton here. *Geronimo Stilton*," I answered.

A female voice giggled sweetly on the other end. "Hi, G! What's squeaking?" she asked.

My snout broke into a broad grin. It was my fascinating friend Petunia Pretty Paws. She is a famouse TV reporter. Petunia has dedicated her life to SAVING THE ENVIRONMENT. What a sweet mouse!

"Hi, Nepunia—I mean, Tenunia—I mean, Petunia," I babbled. Why, oh why, did I turn into such a fool every time I talked to Petunia? She is an amazing mouse. I watch her TV show every night. I have had a huge **CRUSH** on her for the longest time. Too bad I can't even scamper in a straight

line when I'm around her. Still, Petunia is so nice that she never makes fun of me.

"Listen, G. I've got an idea," she said now. "Are you sitting down?"

I grabbed the arms of my chair.

"**Ahem**, yes, I'm not standing. I mean, I'm in my chair. I mean, sitting, check!" I rambled. I clamped my paw over my mouth before Petunia decided to check me into the Mad Mouse Center.

"I need your **help** on my latest assignment," Petunia continued. "We must make a date."

I chewed my whiskers. I loved getting together with Petunia, but I hadn't had my fur cut in weeks. I'd need to make an appointment at Clip Rat's Salon and Day Spa right away. And I could use a sharp new suit. I stared down at the buttons straining on my jacket. I didn't want Petunia to think I was turning into an out-of-shape fur ball.

"**Ahem**, well, how about text Nuesday, I mean, next Tuesday?" I suggested.

Petunia giggled. "I have a better idea," she squeaked. "But first, open the **WINDOW** behind your desk. It's always so stuffy in your office, isn't it?"

I scratched my head. I wasn't sure why Petunia was suddenly interested in climate control, but I did what she asked. I could never say no to Petunia.

I opened the window. A fresh breeze tickled my whiskers. I closed my eyes and took a DEEP BREATH. Ah, my yoga teacher was right. DEEP BREATHING is so wonderful. I felt so refreshed. So energized. So completely

KNOCKED OUT!

You see, before I could say "squeak!" a BLONDE rodent had parachuted in through my window and kicked me right in the snout.

I crumpled like a used Cheesy Chew wrapper. Just before I fainted, I noticed three things: The mouse had shocking BLUE eyes, a tight HOT-PINK jumpsuit, and a look of fearlessness on her pretty face.

Petunia Pretty Paws had landed.

PETUNIA PRETTY PAWS HAS LANDED!

I woke up **STAMMERING**, "Who am I? Where am I? What day is it? What time is it? What's for breakfast? What's for lunch? What's for dinner? I want my mommy!" Just then, somebody slapped me hard in the face.

"G, are you OK? Geronimo, snap out of it!" a voice instructed.

SLAP! SLAP! SLAP!

Are you OK?

I held up my paw. "Please, stop it! Stop slapping me!" I begged. I opened my eyes. Petunia Pretty Paws was staring down at me. A look of concern filled her stunning blue eyes.

"Sorry if I hurt you, G," she squeaked. "But I was worried. You were whining and crying out for your mommy."

I groaned. How embarrassing. Why did I always have to look like such a wimp in front of Petunia?

I flipped my tail behind my back, trying to look cool. It hit my desk with a sickening thud. I whimpered in pain. So much for the macho mouse act.

Meanwhile, Petunia was busy taking off her parachute. She was wearing her trademark **PINK** shirt, jeans, and **brown** belt. An amber necklace hung around her neck. Petunia loved amber gemstones. She collected them on her adventures around the world.

Just then, I had an idea. Not just any idea — a fabumouse idea! Maybe I could buy Petunia something with an amber gemstone in it. Then she'd surely know how much I *liked* her.

I twisted my whiskers, deep in thought. I could buy her a ring. But maybe that was a little too **romantic**. I should probably stick with something like an amber fur comb. Or maybe a cheese knife. What mouse wouldn't love a **beautiful** cheese knife?

I was still thinking about cheese when Petunia **GRABBED** my paw.

"Guess what, G? I brought along a

12

A s-s-s-surprise?

little surprise," she squeaked.

I gulped. "A s-s-s-surprise?" I **stammered**. Last time Petunia surprised me, I almost died of fright. She was doing a show on deadly tornadoes and asked me to come along. We ended up chasing down a **HUMONGOUS** twister. I was so scared, I cried like a baby mouselet the entire trip.

Petunia grinned. "Step aside, G. You're about to meet my brother, wolfgang wild Paws. We call him Wolfie for short," she announced.

I **shook** my head. Petunia had a brother?

Before I could move, I heard a **loud** *WHOOSH* from behind me.

TWO SECONDS LATER, a huge muscular mouse with **BROWN** fur parachuted through the window.

This time, I was struck by the rodent's piercing **BLACK** eyes, watermelon-sized muscles, and **BLUE** steel-toed parachuter's boots. Yep, those boots struck me square on the head.

SMACK!

Once again, I was out like a light.

wolfgang wild Paws

First Name:
Wolfgang

Middle Name:
Wild

Last Name:
Paws

Nickname: Wolfie

Where He Lives: His family has lived for many generations on a farm in the Giant Sequoia Valley, in Dolphin Bay. However, he's always traipsing around the world with his twin sister, Petunia Pretty Paws.

Who He Is: A TV producer who dedicates his life to protecting nature.

His Dream: Saving the environment!

What He Does in His Spare Time: He loves to tell silly stories that nobody else finds funny.

What He Collects: Old geographical maps from around the world.

His Secret: He wants to patent an airplane that runs on clean energy.

Petunia Pretty Paws

First Name:
Petunia

Middle Name:
Pretty

Last Name:
Paws

Nickname: P

Where She Lives: Her family has lived for many generations on a farm in the Giant Sequoia Valley, in Dolphin Bay. However, she's always traipsing around the world with her twin brother, Wolfgang Wild Paws.

Who She Is: A TV reporter who dedicates her life to protecting nature.

Her Dream: Saving the environment!

What She Does in Her Spare Time: She loves to play the flute and hum/sing adorable songs!

What She Collects: Necklaces and amber trinkets from all over the world.

Her Secret: She'd love to marry Geronimo Stilton!

WOLFGANG WILD PAWS HAS LANDED!

When I woke up, the muscle-bound parachuter was **pinching** my tail. Hard.

"You OK there, buddy?!" he shrieked. "Come on, wake up and smell the cheese!"

I blinked. My tail was throbbing. My ears were ringing. And I was getting a giant mouse-sized headache.

"I'd be b-b-b-better," I managed to stammer, "if you'd let go of my tail."

The mouse chuckled. "Oops, guess I don't know my own strength."

Just then, Petunia rushed over. "G, I'd like you to meet my brother, Wolfgang Wild Paws!" she said. "We call him Wolfie."

The big mouse grabbed my **PAW**

and shook it. My bones **crunched**. I wondered if I'd ever write again.

"We have an exciting invitation," Wolfie announced. "We're going to **Australia**, and we want you to come along. You can report on our efforts to save the Australian wildlife and protect the land!"

I chewed my whiskers. Did he say 'wildlife'? I wasn't big on ferocious animals. I tried to explain that I was very busy. In fact, I was in the middle of *writing* a new book. I just had to come up with an iDeA first.

Before I could go on, Petunia grabbed my paw. "Perfect, G! This **trip** will give you tons of ideas!" she squeaked.

Attention!

I opened my mouth to protest when, suddenly, Wolfie flung open the door to my office and **RAN OUT**.

"Attention! Attention!" he squeaked at the top of his lungs. "Mr. Stilton is leaving today for Australia. He will be back in **A MONTH** or **TWO** or **THREE** or **TEN**. Who knows, he may even decide to give up the paper for a more adventurous lifestyle. I mean, who wants to work in a **stuffy** old office? No fresh air. No birds chirping. No warm sun on your fur."

I glanced around. My employees were beginning to look upset.

"Stuffy," I heard someone mumble.

"No sun," another added.

I wanted to **strangle** Wolfie. Everyone looked like they wanted to quit. I had to think **FAST**.

First I explained that I was not leaving the paper. Then I promised to give every worker a weekend gift certificate to The Restful Rodent. Have you ever been there? It's my favorite spa.

I closed my eyes. How I wished I was at The Restful Rodent now. I was still *dreaming* about the spa when two paws grabbed me.

My eyes popped open.

Wolfie was on one side of me. Petunia was on the other.

"No time to sleep, G," Petunia squeaked, smiling at me. "We leave immediately!"

I tried to squeak "wait!" but it was too late. Before I knew what was happening,

they were dragging me away.

We leave immediately!

I Can't See a Thing!

Out on the sidewalk, I noticed Petunia staring at my face intently. Oh, rats. Had I sprouted a pimple?

But Petunia wasn't looking at my fur. She was looking at my glasses.

"Do you really need those glasses, G? Why don't you try taking them off? It's sort of hard to bungee jump and skydive when you're wearing glasses, you know," she said.

I didn't want Petunia to think I was a wimp. But bungee jumping and skydiving weren't exactly on my list of things to do. Did I mention I'm afraid of heights?

I started to explain how much I needed my GLASSES. Too bad Petunia wasn't listening. Before I knew it, she had ripped them off my snout.

I squeaked in protest. Everything had gone blurry. "Give them back!" I shrieked, running around in circles. "You don't understand. I can't see a thing!"

I wasn't lying. I couldn't see my own paw in front of my face. I felt like one of the three blind mice.

"You really can't see me?" Petunia giggled. I nodded at a blurry blob I guessed was my friend.

"Don't **worry**, G," she said in a soothing voice. "I've got a great idea."

I twisted my tail up in a knot. Sometimes Petunia's great ideas turned into my **BIGGEST** nightmares.

Petunia and wolfie took me to the eye doctor. He gave me an eye exam by having me read different letters of the alphabet from a large chart. The letters were bigger at the top and got smaller toward the bottom.

The doctor was very nice. "You're quite nearsighted, but with the right pair of contact lenses, you'll see perfectly." He took out

EYE CONDITIONS

The most common vision problem is **MYOPIA,** or nearsightedness. A myopic person sees objects that are near, well and those that are distant, blurry. **HYPEROPIA**, or farsightedness, is a condition where a person sees objects better from a distance but blurrier when near.

Another vision problem is **ASTIGMATISM**. An astigmatic person sees objects that are both near and far away, distorted. Adults over fifty develop **PRESBYOPIA**. Everything that is near, they see blurry, especially when reading.

two small cases. Inside were two tiny, clear objects. He handed them to me.

"Here are your contact lenses. These will be just right for you. Put them on," he squeaked.

Put them in my *eyes*? I was starting to feel queasy.

"It's easy," the doctor insisted. "Just open your eye wide, and place the lens on your pupil. SIMPLE AS CHEESE PIE!"

Where is it?

①

I opened my eye wide. I put the lens on my pupil. Nothing happened. That's because the lens had fallen on the floor. I searched everywhere for it.

Oops!

When I finally found it, I cleaned it with a special LIQUID. Then I tried again. This time, I poked myself right in the eye.

"Youch!" I screamed.

②

26

I can see!

"Try again," the doctor insisted. "It's **easy**."

I chewed my whiskers. If the doctor said "**easy**" one more time, I just might strangle him.

③

I took a deep breath. *You can do it, Geronimo,* I told myself. And a minute later, I had done it.

I blinked a few times. It was amazing!

"I can see perfectly! Even **better** than when I wear my glasses!" I squeaked.

A minute earlier, I had been ready to choke the doctor. Now I shook his paw.

"Thanks, Doc!" I grinned. I wasn't ready to throw out my glasses just yet. Still, the doctor was right. Putting in contact lenses really was **easy**. Well, with a little practice, of course.

Thanks!

④

A Pair of Verrrry Tight Jeans

Petunia and wolfie walked me home, holding on to my paws. They didn't have to worry. I only tripped twice. And it wasn't because of my new contacts. My sister says I have two left paws.

When we got inside, Petunia told me I needed to pack right away. Wolfie pointed to my clothes. "You're not going to wear that, are you?" he asked in a HORRIFIED tone.

I stared down at my suit. What was wrong with it? It was one of my favorites. And the tie was a present from my dear aunt Sweetfur.

"Do you have a pair of **jeans**?" Petunia asked gently.

I nodded. I knew I had a pair somewhere.

Of course, I hadn't worn them in a million years. . . .

I dug through my **dresser**, my **closet**, and looked under my **bed**.

"They've got to be here somewhere," I muttered. Finally, I found a pair. The only problem was that I couldn't fit into them.

"These jeans got **too tight!**" I cried.

"Or maybe you ate too **MANY** double-decker cheese sandwiches," Wolfie said with a smirk.

I forced myself to ignore him. So I liked to

Geronimo when he was ten years old.

Geronimo when he was twenty years old.

Geronimo today!

drink a few mozzarella milk shakes at night. So what? It wasn't against the law.

I gripped the jeans with determination. Then I held my breath, and **zipped**.

"Wow, G. Those look **skintight**. Are you sure they're comfortable?" Petunia asked.

I plastered a smile on my face.

"**Ahem**, certainly, I feel great," I choked. *Breathing is overrated,* I chanted softly to myself.

Just then, I heard my tummy rumble. I realized I was starving. I scarfed down

three **cheddar** sandwiches in the blink of an eye. After I was done, I was ready to **burst**.

I had to get out of the jeans! There was only one little PROBLEM. They were stuck to me like glue!

Petunia leaped into action. She grabbed another sandwich.

"**EAT iT!**" she ordered.

I opened my mouth to complain. Wrong move. *QUICK* as a cat, Petunia shoved the sandwich down my throat. A minute later, the zipper on the jeans burst open. Buttons began **POPPING** off my shirt in every direction. I could move! I could breathe! I was saved!

Arghhh!

WHERE ARE YOU GOING, GERONIMO?

As the last button popped, my doorbell rang.

I opened the door. It was my **family**. Their jaws dropped when they saw my suitcases.

"Where are you going, Geronimo?!" they squeaked in unison.

My cousin Trap pointed to my split jeans. "New look, Germeister?" he said, **smirking**.

My grandfather William put his paw in the air for SILENCE.

"**QUIET**, everyone!" he thundered. "I want an explanation, Grandson! What's this I hear about you selling the newspaper? Has the cheese slipped off your cracker?"

I tried to explain.

"Don't worry, everyone. Everything is OK. I'm not leaving the newspaper. I'm just going on a short trip to Australia with my friend Petunia Pretty Paws and her brother, Wolfie," I said.

"Australia?" Trap squeaked.

"Wolfie?!" Grandfather William exploded. "What kind of a name is Wolfie?!"

Wolfie gave my grandfather a shoulder-breaking slap on his back. "It's short for Wolfgang, Grandpappy. Or should I call you Pops?" He chuckled.

Should I call you Pops?

I winced. Steam poured out of Grandfather William's ears. He looked like he was ready to explode.

No one messes with Grandfather William and gets away with it.

Putrid cheese puffs! If my family didn't leave soon, things could get ugly. I thanked everyone for coming and pushed them out the door.

Let's go, G!

My family was still in sight when Petunia appeared before me with a new pair of jeans.

"They're Wolfie's," she explained. "Put them on. Then we're out of here!"

Ten minutes later, we arrived at the airport.

A Very Unusual Continent . . .

As soon as we boarded the plane, I buckled and unbuckled my seat belt ten times. Then I checked to make sure I had my chewing gum, nose spray, aspirin, and Cheeseball the Clown doll.

Did I mention I'm afraid to fly?

Luckily, Petunia gave me a book to read. It was called **A Guide to Australia**.

"It's going to be long flight," she said. "Australia is on the other side of the world, so you'll have plenty of time to look through this book."

I began reading it. It was really **INTERESTING**. Australia is truly a very unusual **CONTINENT**!

TIMOR SEA

ARAFURA SEA

CORAL SEA

GREAT BARRIER REEF

INDIAN OCEAN

Hamersley Range

MacDonnell Range

Great Dividing Range

PACIFIC OCEAN

Great Victoria Desert

INDIAN OCEAN

AUSTRALIA

AREA: 2,967,909 square miles

POPULATION: 20,090,437

BORDERS: Surrounded on the north by the Timor and Arafura seas, on the northeast by the Coral Sea, on the east by the Pacific Ocean, and on the south and west by the Indian Ocean.

CAPITAL: Canberra

TYPE OF GOVERNMENT: Democratic federation of states. The head of state is the king or queen of England.

LANGUAGE: English, and many indigenous languages spoken by the Aborigines.

MONEY: Australian dollar

CLIMATE: Generally, warmer and drier than the United States. Most of the continent gets only 5 to 20 inches of rain per year. Parts of the northeast get 60 inches of rain per year.

GERONIMO'S TRIP TO AUSTRALIA

Darwin

Port Hedland

Shark Bay

Uluru
(Ayers Rock

Perth

N
W   E
S

Key
International flight
Domestic flight
Traveled by jeep

Alice Springs

Brisbane

Adelaide

Sydney

Canberra

Melbourne

Hobart

AUSTRALIA

Australia is the smallest of the seven continents, and the only one that is a country in itself. People sometimes call it the "Land Down Under" because it lies entirely in the Southern Hemisphere. Winter in Australia is from June to August and summer is from December to February. It's about the size of the United States without Alaska and Hawaii. Australia formed more than 50 million years ago, separating itself from the other continents. That is why its animals and plants are so different. And because Australia is so old, it is the lowest and flattest continent, with vast deserts, beaches, mountains, and rain forests.

THE FIRST AUSTRALIANS

Humans probably arrived in Australia more than 40,000 years ago from Southeast Asia. They lived in groups, forming many different tribes, who spoke many different languages. The people survived by moving from place to place, hunting and gathering food. They lived in huts or caves. Later immigrants from Europe called these nomads Aborigines.

CAPTAIN JAMES COOK

Some Europeans began to explore the coast of Australia in the 17th century. Captain James Cook landed in Botany

Bay, south of present-day Sydney in 1770. He claimed the eastern coastland for England, naming it New South Wales. In 1788, the first settlers arrived from Great Britain. They were mostly convicts, soldiers, and government officials. By 1830, Great Britain claimed the entire continent. People from England and Ireland went to Australia to grow wheat and raise sheep.

More than 40,000 years ago The first humans arrive in Australia from Asia.

1770 Captain Cook lands in Botany Bay.

1788 The English begin to colonize Australia.

1901 Australia becomes independent.

1945–1965 People from Italy, Greece, the Middle East, Vietnam, and Hong Kong begin to live in Australia.

THE COMMONWEALTH OF AUSTRALIA

Australia became a commonwealth, an independent nation within the British Empire, on January 1, 1901. The king or queen of England is the official head of the state, but is represented by the governor-general in Australia. It is a democratic federation of six states and two territories.

TOPOGRAPHY

Australia has four main land areas: the Coastal Plain along the south and east, where most people live; the Eastern Highlands, which includes the Great Dividing Range; the Central-Eastern Lowlands, which has the best land for farming along the Murray and Durling Rivers; and the Great Western Plateau, which is generally known as the Outback.

The Great Barrier Reef

The Great Barrier Reef is the largest area of coral reefs and islands in the world. Situated off the northeastern coast of Australia, it stretches for about 1,250 miles. The reef is home to 400 species of coral, 1,500 species of tropical fish

The Golden Wattle

The golden wattle (*Acacia pycnantha*) is the national flower of Australia. The shrub has broad, bright green leaves and fluffy, yellow, sweet-smelling flowers that bloom around September 1—National Wattle Day.

(including the wobbegong, a little gray-and-brown shark), 16 species of sea snake, and 6 species of sea turtle.

The Coastal Plain

Australians live on a strip of land along the eastern and southern coasts of the continent called the Coastal Plain. It contains lush tropical areas and dry, sandy plains. The climate is warm and moist, and the farmland is rich.

The Outback

The interior of Australia is also called the Outback. Mostly desert, it also features vast cattle and sheep stations, ancient mountain ranges, and red-baked earth. Watch out for kangaroos hopping through the bush, camels, and emus.

Eucalyptus Eucalyptus trees are the most common trees in Australia. They are able to survive fire, dry spells, and poor soil. Eucalyptus leaves are the only food koalas will eat. These sleepy koalas love to nap in the branches of eucalyptus trees.

Taipan The taipan is one of the most poisonous snakes in the world! It lives in the northern part of the continent and can grow to be 10 feet long.

A SIGHT FOR SORE EYES

After traveling for what felt like ten million hours, we finally LANDED in Sydney. Well, OK, maybe it wasn't that long. Still, Sydney was a sight for sore eyes. It is the biggest city in Australia. I could see the Opera House, a spectacular building with a roof shaped just like the sails on a boat.

JET LAG occurs when a person flies to a new time zone. The body's biological clock is out of sync with the local time. You might have a headache or a stomachache, feel tired or thirsty. It usually takes one day to recover for each time zone you cross.

New York
7:15 A.M.

London
12:15 P.M.

Cairo
2:15 P.M.

Sydney
11:15 P.M.

I calculated the difference in time zones from Mouse Island. Then I called my little nephew Benjamin.

"I'm in Australia," I said. Benjamin's excited squeak nearly pierced my eardrum. Youch!

YOU CAN DO IT!

Wolfie decided we should hit Bondi Beach first. It is the most famous beach in Sydney. The water was a breathtaking turquoise color, and the sand was warm and squishy. What a perfect place for a nice quiet mousenap. Unfortunately, Wolfie had other ideas.

He INSISTED I put on a pair of tight, stretchy shorts. Then he practically clonked me over the head with a surfboard.

I put on a pair of tight, stretchy shorts.

He clonked me over the head with a surfboard.

The next thing I knew, he had me *swimming* out to sea. I lay on the surfboard on my tummy, paddling desperately with my paws.

The waves were **HUMONGOUS**. I was scared out of my fur!

"Now catch a **wave** and ride it, G! It will bring you back to shore!" Wolfie shouted.

Ride a wave? **WAS HE NUTS?** I could barely ride a tricycle!

Wolfie must have seen the look of sheer terror in my eyes. "You can do it!" he yelled. "Besides, you're better off riding the waves than staying here. Sharks love these waters."

I was paddling desperately with my paws.

I was scared out of my fur!

I broke out in a fit of sobs. Then I spotted the most enormouse wave ever, and it was headed straight toward me! *Snap out of it, Geronimo,* I scolded myself. *If you don't ride this wave, you'll end up a dead rat in some slimy shark's belly!*

With a burst of strength, I mounted the surfboard, and rode the wave in. It was so hard to **balance**! I ended up doing some crazy acrobatics trying not to fall off. When I came to shore, all of the rodents at the beach applauded.

I couldn't believe it. I, Geronimo Stilton, was a surfing *sensation*!

I love to eat mice. Yum-yum!

GOOD-BYE,
RODENTS!

We decided to check out another beach. First we had to **get on** a plane. Rats! Then we had to take a LONG, LONG bus ride.

When we got to the beach, Wolfie told me to dive right in. I was feeling **CONFIDENT** after my surfing debut, so I did.

"Get ready for a surprise!" Wolfie called.

I looked around in a panic. A surprise? In the water?

That's when I noticed a sign back on the beach. It read:

My stomach lurched. My whiskers trembled. Oh, why did I have such horrible luck? I was a good mouse. I never bothered anyone. Well, except for that time I asked a church mouse to stop ringing the bells. I couldn't help it. They were giving

SHARK!!

me an awful **HEADACHE**.

Just then, I saw a fin approaching.

"**SHARK!**" I shrieked at the top of my lungs.

I began swimming like a madmouse. The fin came **closer** and **closer**. It caught up with me!

I closed my eyes. *This is it,* I told myself. "Good-bye, rodents everywhere!" I sobbed. But nothing happened.

Well, something did happen. A soft snout poked me in the back.

I opened my eyes and saw . . . a dolphin!

Then I felt sprays all around me. **Splash! Splash! Splash! Splash!**

It was Petunia and Wolfie. "Come on, G, let's swim with the dolphins!" they shouted.

The dolphins were happy to have new friends. They let us **get on** their backs as they swam around. It was unbelievable.

As soon as I got out of the water, I called my nephew Benjamin.

I told him all about our incredible afternoon. This time, Benjamin's excited squeak reminded me of our new friends, the dolphins.

A 600-MILLION-YEAR-OLD ROCK

Can you guess what we did next? Yep, we took another plane. Good thing I thought ahead and packed a few emergency air sickness bags. Oh, how I hate to fly!

Finally, we arrived in a place called Alice Springs. There we boarded a jeep and took a long drive through the **DUSTY** desert.

At **SUNSET**, we stopped. I was so relieved. Have you ever ridden in a jeep? My tail was sore from all those bumps.

I was about to tumble out of the jeep when Petunia squeaked excitedly and grabbed my paw. She pointed to an immense red mountain on the horizon.

I recognized it from the guidebook. It was **ULURU**.

ULURU
Uluru, previously known as Ayers Rock, is the largest exposed rock in the world. It is 1,141 feet high, 2.2 miles long, and 1.2 miles wide. Formed nearly 600 million years ago, this red sandstone monolith is considered a sacred place by its Aborigine owners—the Anangu people—and is part of a World Heritage site.

A RED GLOWING ROCK

I forgot about my sore tail. I was too excited. We drove to the base of the immense red mountain in the middle of a **DESERT**. What an amazing place! Uluru seemed to glow in the setting sun.

We all stared silently at the beautiful sight. It was **magical**.

Then a group of rowdy tourists drove up. They **climbed** out of their jeeps. They were

so noisy I could hardly hear myself think.

"Hey, dudes, let's scale this mountain!" one of them yelled.

click
click

"Bring the camera!" another one shouted.

click

I felt sad. Our magical place didn't seem so magical anymore.

click
click
click

Just then, a rodent approached us.

click

He had dark fur and a thick, *CURLY* black beard. "Will you also be climbing the mountain?" he asked us.

I turned around and saw a different group of rodents. They all had dark fur. I realized they must be ABORIGINES.

Petunia's guidebook said that the Aborigines were descendants of the first people who lived in Australia. Their culture was truly *fascinating*.

Then I remembered something else I had read in the guidebook. It said

The Aborigines of that area, the Anangu, call any tourist who tries to climb Uluru *minga* (ant). The Anangu would prefer that people do not climb to the top. The route is sacred to them and they feel responsible for the visitors' safety. They offer tourists a walking tour around the base with an Aborigine guide to explain their history and culture.

that the Aborigines felt the **mountain** was sacred. I knew they would not want STRANGERS climbing it.

"No, sir. We will not go on top of Uluru," I answered. "We respect your wishes."

Petunia and Wolfie nodded.

"We don't need to take any photos, either," Petunia added.

"pictures

cannot capture the special feeling of this place!"

The Aborigines

People began living in Australia 40,000 to 60,000 years ago. When the Europeans first settled the continent in 1788, there were between 300,000 to 1 million natives living in tribes. Each tribe had its own language and its own territory. The colonists called the natives Aborigines. The Aborigines lived in complete harmony with the land, the animals, and the plants. They moved from place to place to find food and water with the changing seasons.

Totem

Each Aborigine tribe has its own totem. The totem can be a plant, an animal, a bird, or a rock. This sacred symbol never changes and supposedly was chosen by the tribe's ancestral beings. It plays a very important role in the tribe's spiritual and social life.

Corroboree

Aborigines often celebrate important events in their lives with a corroboree. This nocturnal celebration can be an initiation ceremony in which everyone performs, or a sacred event for a few people in the tribe. As part of the festival, the people wear special costumes and play musical instruments such as didgeridoos, rattles, and sticks.

YOU ARE WELCOME IN OUR LAND

The rodent with the beard stared at us for a **long** time. I couldn't read his expression under all that fur. Was he happy? Was he sad? Was he looking for a good place for dinner? I know *I* was. I was starving. I hadn't eaten anything since that bag of stale cheese crisps on the plane. Right then, my tummy rumbled loudly.

Now the other Aborigines were staring at me, too. I was so **embarrassed**. For a moment, no one said squeak. Then everyone burst out laughing.

Wolfie slapped me on the back. Hard. "Oh, G, we can't take you anywhere!" he teased.

Geronimo Stilton

The rodent with the beard grinned. He BOWED his head in greeting. "You are welcome in our land, foreigners," he said.

I introduced myself. "My name is Stilton, *Geronimo Stilton*," I said. I told him I was the publisher of *The Rodent's Gazette.* I was going to add that it was the most popular **newspaper** on Mouse Island, but I hate to brag.

Petunia and Wolfie shook the Aborigine's paw. "I'm Petunia, and this is my brother, Wolfgang Paws. We are doing research on Australia. Our mission is to protect NATURE and save the environment in every corner of the world!" Petunia said.

I sighed. Isn't she the most amazing mouse? Petunia is so

Petunia Pretty Paws

Wolfgang Wild Paws

passionate about her work. I stared at her dreamily.

My thoughts were interrupted by the Aborigine's excited squeak.

"I know who you are!" He *beamed* at Petunia. "Your TV show on **PROTECTING NATURE** is famouse here!"

The Aborigine said his name was **WANGARA**. He was the chief of the Anangu people. His wife's name was **WANI**.

"We would like to film a **DOCUMENTARY** showing the public the wonders of the bush country. Will you help us?" Petunia asked.

Wani

Wangara nodded his head excitedly. "It would be my honor," he squeaked.

This time when we boarded

the jeep, we had two extra passengers, Wangara and Wani.

"Ready for more ADVENTURE, G?" Wolfie asked. Then he slapped me on the back with his PAW. Hard.

I would have answered, but I was too busy trying to catch my breath. He had knocked the wind out of me.

An emu is an Australian ostrich. It's more than 6 feet tall.

The kookaburra's call sounds like it's laughing.

A kangaroo can jump 25 feet, using its tail as a rudder.

An echidna may look like a porcupine, but it's an egg-laying marsupial.

In Australia, the bush describes the parts of the country that are wilderness. The land is uncultivated and wild, far from cities or towns where people live.

A koala sleeps almost 20 hours a day and only eats eucalyptus leaves.

A dingo is a wild dog that doesn't bark, but it does howl.

A platypus is a furry, warm-blooded mammal that lays eggs and hunts underwater.

HUGE SPIDERS AND EXTREMELY POISONOUS SNAKES!

We drove through the Australian bush. All different types of trees, bushes, and plants surrounded us. We saw tall eucalyptus trees, horsetails, acacias, and ceibas. Noisy birds called kookaburras squawked to us from high above.

We parked our jeep at the edge of the forest.

"Let's leave the car here and travel on foot," Wangara

Wangara

instructed. "This way, you can reconnect with the land. We Aborigines respect nature and have learned to live in harmony with it. That's because nature supplies us with everything we need. The warmth of the sun, the air we breathe, the water we drink, the fruit we eat, and the animals that dwell in the forest — *nature is our friend*. But you must be very careful. The forest is also filled with danger."

I shivered. I loved nature, but the danger part I could do without.

Slowly, we began to make our way through

Wani

Youch!

the bush. I had only taken a few steps when my paw felt a stabbing pain. **Youch!** What had I stepped on?

"**ECHIDNA**," Wangara squeaked. "It's an animal with very long, sharp quills."

Very sharp? Those quills were *razor-sharp*! While I was still jumping around in pain, I bumped into something. It gave me a blinding kick with its muscular leg.

Wani giggled. "**KANGAROO**," she informed us. "It is very famous for its powerful kicks."

Oops!

Powerful kicks? This thing must have had a black belt in karate! I sat down to catch my breath.

Heeeelp!

Big mistake. I had plopped down on a huge egg. An enormous bird flew at me and began pecking me on the head.

Wangara murmured, "**EMU.** It lays gigantic green eggs."

Terrified, I batted the bird away. I fell against a tree trunk, exhausted. That's when I felt something near my legs.

Wani ran worriedly toward me. "Taipan! It's one of the most poisonous snakes in the whole world!" she yelled.

What's happening?

Chilled to the paw, I couldn't help imagining the snake wrapping itself around me! I managed to stand completely frozen until the taipan slithered away. By

HELPFUL HINTS ON HOW
TO SURVIVE IN THE BUSH

1. Bring lots and lots of water with you. If you finish it before going to sleep, hang a plastic bag on a tree branch. Put the branch leaves inside the bag, then tie it tightly around the branch. By the following morning, you'll find water in the plastic bag!

2. Don't forget to bring a map, a compass to find your bearings, and a whistle. If you get lost in the bush, you could always call for help by using the whistle.

3. If you make camp, don't litter. Nature needs to be respected. Remember that animals could smell your garbage and enter your campsite.

4. When you venture into the bush, always bring food with you. If you plan to stay in the bush for several days, you can make some Australian bush bread — damper. It is a bread traditionally baked in the coals of an open fire. (See recipe on page 83.)

now, my nerves were shot. I could not take another step.

When Wangara pointed to a spot on the ground, I nearly jumped out of my fur. "What is it?" I cried. "Does it STING? Does it BITE? Is it a huge spider?!" Then I began

sobbing uncontrollably.

"Don't worry, Geronimo," Wani soothed me. "We just wanted to show you the wild pumpkins growing right under your feet."

Wild Pumpkin

I blushed. Oh, why did I always have to make such a fool of myself?

Next, Wani showed us some orange-colored nuts. "Wow!" I said, popping a few in my mouth. "I didn't know macadamias grew wild in Australia."

Macadamias

She also pointed to lots of honeycombs hanging from tree branches. "We Aborigines use honey instead of sugar," Wangara explained.

That night around the fire, while eating some damper bread that Wani had baked, Wangara told us a beautiful Aborigine legend about the

Honeycombs

Dreamtime . . .

During the Dreamtime, the Earth was silent. Nothing grew and nothing moved. All the animals slept under the ground. Then one day, the Rainbow Snake, Mother of Life, woke up and headed toward the surface. She looked around and began to wander here and there. The surface of the Earth became furrowed, marked by the traces left by her body. After the Rainbow Snake had slithered throughout the entire Earth, she returned to where she came from and called to the frogs, "Come out!"

The frogs came out slowly because their bellies were filled with water that was stored there during their long sleep. The Rainbow Snake began tickling their tummies until they laughed so much that the water spilled out and filled the furrows left by the Rainbow Snake on the dirt, thus forming rivers and lakes.

Then the grass
began to grow and trees
began to sprout. All of the animals, birds,
and reptiles woke up and followed the Rainbow
Snake. They were happy, and everyone survived
by hunting for food to feed their tribe. In time,
the Rainbow Snake made laws that not everyone
respected. So the Rainbow Snake said, "Those who
follow my rules will be well rewarded. They, their
children, and their children's children will live
on this land forever and ever. This will be their
land. Those who do not follow my rules will be
punished. They will never walk on this land again."

Not everyone obeyed the rules. So the Rainbow
Snake kept order, punishing some and rewarding
others. From then on, the tribes lived together on
the land, knowing that no one would ever take
it away from them and that it would be theirs
forever.

Heeeeelp! I Don't Want to be Left Aloooooooone!

The following morning, I woke up at the crack of dawn. Someone—or something—was SCREECHING in my ear. My heart thudded under my fur. My paws started to sweat.

"D-d-d-don't hurt me!" I yelped. Then I opened my eyes. A kookaburra stared down at me from a nearby eucalyptus tree.

"Ahem, well, good morning," I said to the bird, feeling foolish. Luckily, no one was around to see me. Where was everyone?

"Hello?!" I called out.

No one answered. I looked around, confused. There was no one in sight.

I was all alone.

The color DRAINED from my fur. I felt weak. I felt dizzy. I felt faint. Rats! I was about to have a full-out panic attack. I slumped down onto a tree trunk.

"Somebody, help!" I squeaked faintly.

Oh, how did I get myself into such a mess? Headlines *FLASHED* before my eyes: "STILTON LOST IN THE AUSTRALIAN BUSH! PUBLISHER BITES THE DUST ON ASSIGNMENT!"

I pulled out my wallet and stared at pictures of my family. There was my obnoxious cousin, Trap, my sister, Thea, and Grandfather William. Last but not least, I pulled out my nephew Benjamin's school picture. His sweet face smiled up at me.

Suddenly, I felt a surge of energy. *I would not give up.* I had to make it back for my dear sweet nephew. He thought I was the best thing since SLICED CHEESE.

Quickly, I packed up my backpack and began **walking**. I remembered what Wangara had told me: "To go back to Uluru, you need to follow the direction of the setting sun." That meant west.

I walked for ten million *hours*. Well, OK, maybe only for three hours, but it sure felt longer. I was exhausted. I picked a wild pumpkin, then some nuts and fruit. I grabbed a honeycomb from a tree. The bees were furious! I dove into a nearby swamp to escape. Putrid cheese puffs, that was a close call!

WHEN YOU'RE HUNGRY . . . EVERYTHING TASTES DELICIOUS!

When it got dark, I stopped at a clearing. I needed to make a fire. I tried and tried. Nothing happened. Rats! I knew I should have paid more attention as a rodent scout.

Just as I was about to give up, I saw a **spark**. The dry grass caught fire. "I did it!" I shrieked. But no one was around to hear me.

Even so, the fire cheered me up. It flickered brightly in the night. I felt **WARM** and cozy. I cooked the wild pumpkin I had picked during the day. I tried the fruit, **nuts**, and a piece of the damper that we had made the night before. Then I sucked on the drippings from the HONEYCOMB.

It was a strange meal. Still I was happy. I guess, when you're HUNGRY, everything

Damper: Australian Bush Bread

1-1/4 to 1-1/2 cups milk
4 cups all-purpose flour
2 tablespoons baking powder
4 teaspoons sugar
2 tablespoons butter

1. Preheat oven to 400°F. Ask an adult to help.
2. Sift the all-purpose flour, baking powder, and salt into a large mixing bowl. Mix in sugar.
3. Using a pastry blender, put the butter into the flour mixture until it resembles crumbs. Or you can rub the butter into the mixture using your fingertips.
4. Make a well in the center of the flour mixture. Pour in 1-1/4 cups of milk. Using a wooden spoon, mix well until the mixture pulls away from the sides of the bowl.

Add up to 1/4 cup more milk, if necessary.
5. Turn the dough out onto a well-floured board and knead until smooth. Shape into a mounded loaf about 7 inches around and about 2 inches thick. Place on a greased cookie sheet and cut across 1/2 inch deep on top of the loaf.
6. Bake for 25 minutes. Lower temperature to 375° F. Bake 10 to 15 minutes longer until the bread is golden in color and sounds hollow when tapped. Makes one 7- to 8-inch loaf.

tastes *delicious*!

After I ate, I rubbed my tummy. A loud burp escaped me. I giggled. Normally, I would have been totally mortified. After all, I am a gentlemouse. But tonight, I didn't care. No one could hear me! I snorted with laughter.

Suddenly, a voice called out from the DARK woods. "Having fun, Geronimo?"

I jumped so high my whiskers hit the leaves of a eucalyptus tree.

Four **mysterious** shadows crept out of the bushes. My fur turned beet red. It was my friends Petunia, Wolfie, Wangara, and Wani! I was so happy. I was so relieved. I was so furious. A million questions raced through my head.

"Why did you leave me alone?" I squeaked. "I could have been bitten by a poisonous snake! What if I was kicked by a crazed kangaroo?

I could have eaten a bad berry and . . ."

Wangara stopped me before I could go on. "We left you alone to teach you a lesson," he said solemnly.

"We wanted you to see you could survive on your own in the bush," Wani added.

Petunia put her paw around me. "I knew you could do it, G! We're all so proud," she cheered.

I couldn't believe my ears. Everyone was proud of me? I puffed up my fur. Maybe I wasn't such a 'fraidy mouse after all.

Before I knew it, I was in the center of a **warm** group hug. I was feeling so special. So loved. So squished. Wolfie was crushing every bone in my body!

We're so proud!

GIFTS FROM THE HEART

When everyone was done **hugging**, Wangara stepped forward. He held out what looked like a musical instrument.

"This is a didgeridoo. It was made from the branches of the eucalyptus tree," he explained. "My grandfather gave it to me when I was little. Now I want you to have it. It is a *gift* from the bottom of my heart."

I was so touched. I could tell the didgeridoo meant the world to Wangara.

I racked my brain. What could I give him in return? It had to be something very special.

> The **didgeridoo** is a large trumpet made from the branches of the eucalyptus tree. It is usually decorated with typical Aboriginal designs. Traditionally, only men play this instrument.

Not just a box of Cheesy Chews. Although they are extra tasty.

Just then, I had an idea. I took out the fountain pen my grandfather William Shortpaws had given me when I was little. Now that was something special. I wrote down some of my best ideas with that pen.

Wangara as a small child

"This is a fountain pen. It was a present from my grandfather, too. I want you to have it," I said.

Wangara smiled. Even though we didn't have the same traditions, I could tell my new friend understood that it was an important gift.

Geronimo as a mouselet

Sweet, Sweet, New Mouse City . . .

Soon, it was time to leave. We said good-bye to Wangara and Wani. I knew I would never forget them. And I would never forget all of my *adventures* in Australia. It was a **FABUMOUSE** place.

We boarded the plane and took off **FOR HOME**. Ah, home, sweet home. Don't get me wrong, I loved Australia. But I was still missing my beloved Mouse Island. Plus, I was dying to sink my teeth into a cheesy burrito at Hotfur's Mexican Cantina. **YUM!**

Attention: Geronimo Stilton is aboard this plane on his way home!

YOU NEVER STOP LEARNING

Onboard the plane, Petunia, Wolfie and I talked about **ALL** of the things we had learned in Australia.

"No matter how old you get, you never stop learning," said Petunia. She was right!

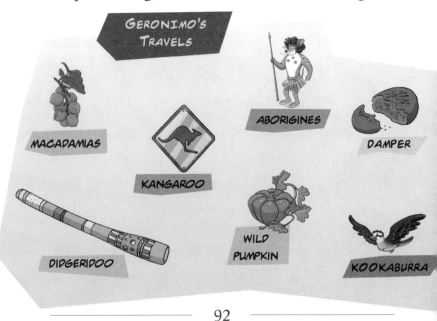

GERONIMO'S TRAVELS

MACADAMIAS

KANGAROO

ABORIGINES

DAMPER

DIDGERIDOO

WILD PUMPKIN

KOOKABURRA

No matter how old you get, you never stop learning!

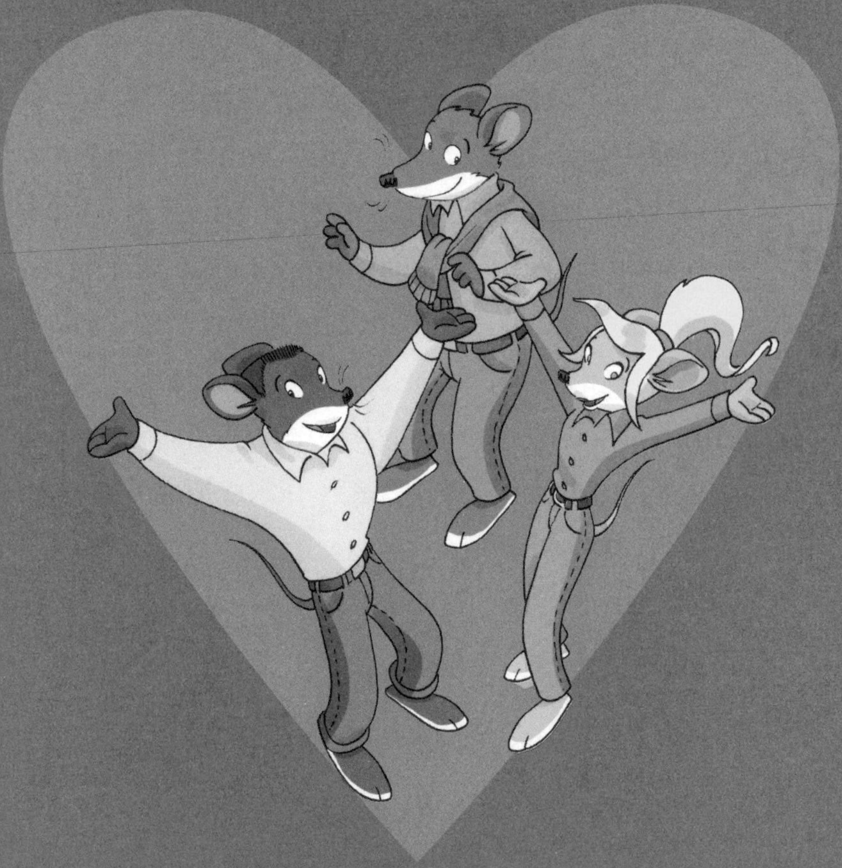

GIANT SEQUOIA VALLEY

The next morning, I was relaxing in my comfy mouse hole when the phone rang. It was Petunia.

"G, I just had a great idea. Wolfie and I are taking a little trip to the Paws Family Farm. Why don't you come with us?" she suggested.

I blinked. Didn't these rodents ever rest?

I was still **exhausted** from our last trip. I had a ton of laundry to do. And my fridge had a yummy cheddar sandwich with my name on it. Too bad I could never say no to Petunia.

Before I knew it, I was sitting in a jeep headed for the Paws Family Farm. We **CROSSED** through a forest of extremely tall trees.

"This is **Giant** Sequoia Valley," Petunia explained. "They are the oldest trees in the world."

Before long, we reached a WROUGHT-IRON gate. There were large black letters above it that read **PAWS**.

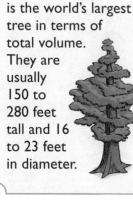

The Giant Sequoia is the world's largest tree in terms of total volume. They are usually 150 to 280 feet tall and 16 to 23 feet in diameter.

Wolfie punched in a code. Then we drove up a long red dirt path.

At last, we reached a huge house. Petunia knocked on the door.

"Open up! It's us! We're HOME!" she announced.

The door opened a crack. A rodent's snout peeked out. She was **very, very** old and petite. She gave us a warm smile.

"Grandma Paws!" my friends shouted, wrapping her in a hug.

THE PAWS FARM

I winced. I hoped Wolfie didn't SQUEEZE her too tightly. Grandma looked so frail she might break in two like a cheese stick.

"My dearest grandchildren! It's so wonderful to see you again! Where in the world did you come from this time?" Grandma exclaimed.

HE'S PERFECT FOR YOU, PETUNIA!

Petunia and Wolfie told Grandmother Paws about our adventure in Australia. Then she turned to me.

"And who is this young mouse?" she asked.

I stepped forward and gently shook her paw.

"**Ahem**, so pleased to meet you. My name is *Geronimo Stilton*. I am the publisher of *The Rodent's Gazette*. Petunia and I are

Pleased to meet you!

Oooh!

dear friends," I explained.

Grandmother Paws grinned. She told me she loved my newspaper. Then she winked at Petunia. "He's smart. And he's a gentlemouse," she squeaked. "He's perfect for you, Petunia!"

I blushed right up to my whiskers.

Luckily, Petunia didn't seem to notice. "Thanks for the advice, Grandma," she giggled.

Grandmother Paws showed me around the house. She offered to set up the guest room for me. But I told her I had to get back home. My family had planned a special welcome-home dinner. They wanted to hear all about my adventures in Australia.

"Well, you must at least taste my fresh lemonade and try a few chocolate-cheesy-chip cookies," Grandma insisted.

It's so delicious!

Chocolate-cheesy-chip-cookies? How could I say no?

We all sat together in the warm cozy Paws family kitchen. The **AROMA** of freshly baked cookies filled the air.

"Cookie, Geronimo?" Grandma asked.

I tried nibbling just one. But Grandma's cookies were so yummy, I couldn't stop myself. Before I knew it, I had scarfed down another and another. I guess all that time in the bush had given me a new appreciation for home-baked goods.

Just then, I noticed Petunia staring at me. Oh, why had I made such a pig of myself?

 Luckily, I was saved by my cell phone. It was my nephew Benjamin. He wanted to know when I was coming home. I smiled. "I will see everyone tonight at the FAMILY DINNER."

"A family mouse, too. What a catch!" Grandma squeaked.

Then she showed me a photo album. "Even though we have a big family, we are very close," she explained. "In fact, there are Paws all over the WORLD!"

Finally, it was time for me to go. Wolfie took me out back. He pointed to a helicopter parked on a grassy landing pad. "It's your lucky day, Geronimo. I'm going to take you home in my brand-new 'copter. I just got my pilot's license," he squeaked.

I was scared furless. But what could I do? I had to get home. My family was waiting for me. I hugged Petunia good-bye.

"It was great traveling with you, G. I hope we'll get to go on another adventure real soon," she whispered.

THE PAWS FAMILY

Bugsy Wugsy Daughter of John and Furry. She is nine years old and wants to save the environment like her aunt Petunia.

Slugsy Wugsy Son of John and Furry. He is Bugsy's dreadful little brother and can never sit still!

Lilly, Lally, and Lolly Paws Daughters of Lucy and Tom. Lilly is five years old and adores helping her mother in the garden. Lally is seven years old and loves horseback riding. Lolly is eleven years old and is nuts about traveling, just like Grandmother Paws.

Lucy Valley Tom's wife. She has a passion for growing all kinds of flowers, plants, fruits, and vegetables.

Tom Paws Son of Teddy and Jenny. He adores working with his father and has inherited a passion for natural sciences from his grandfather.

John Wugsy Furry's husband. He loves living in the country and taking long bicycle rides with Petunia.

Furry Paws Daughter of Bobby and Suzy, sister to Petunia and Wolfie. She's Bugsy and Slugsy's mother.

Suzy Rattella Bobby Paws's wife. She has a passion for dolphins and works for the Marine Center in New Mouse City.

Bobby Paws Son of Grandfather and Grandmother Paws. He runs the Paws Farm with his brother, Teddy.

Wolfgang Wild Paws Son of Bobby and Suzy, and twin brother to Petunia. He is a TV producer and travels all over the world to save the environment.

Petunia Pretty Paws Daughter of Bobby and Suzy, she's Wolfie's twin sister. She is a TV reporter and travels all over the world to save the environment.

Jenny Littlepaw Teddy's wife. She's an exceptional cook. The entire Paws family adores her Sweet Tooth Cake!

Teddy Paws Son of Grandfather and Grandmother Paws. He runs the Paws Farm along with his brother, Bobby.

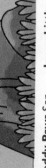

Grandmother Paws As a young mouselet, she traveled all over the world when airplanes were not yet in existence.

Grandfather Paws Well-versed in natural sciences, he once traveled the world in search of a very rare butterfly.

THAT'S ANOTHER STORY . . .

I boarded the helicopter with shaky paws. My heart was thumping **a mile a minute**. My tail was twisted up in a knot. Oh, how I hate to fly!

Wolfie didn't notice. He **chattered** away as the helicopter lifted into the air.

"You know, G, Petunia and I are going on another trip next month. Maybe you'd like to join us. We're going to the Mousehara Desert. I want to do a documentary on **SCORPIONS**. I need someone to help me test which ones are the most poisonous. What do you think?" he babbled.

Scorching hot desert? Deadly scorpions?

Normally, I would have been horrified. But right then, I noticed Petunia standing on the runway waving at me. I felt my heart melt. I don't know what it is about Petunia, but for some reason she could always get me to do the most OUTRAGEOUS things. She was so kind and beautiful and brave and caring.

Have a safe trip!

I grinned. Maybe I could handle a few scorpions if I was with Petunia. But that's another story . . .

Want to read my next adventure?
It's sure to be a fur-raising experience!

THE MOUSE ISLAND MARATHON

I admit it — I'm not much of a muscle mouse. So when I accidentally got signed up for the Mouse Island Marathon, I was so shocked that I lost my squeak! Me, run a marathon? But my friends and family were determined to help me cross that finish line. Holey cheese, I was never going to make it!

ABOUT THE AUTHOR

 Born in New Mouse City, Mouse Island, Geronimo Stilton is Rattus Emeritus of Mousomorphic Literature and of Neo-Ratonic Comparative Philosophy. For the past twenty years, he has been running *The Rodent's Gazette*, New Mouse City's most widely read daily newspaper.

Stilton was awarded the Ratitzer Prize for his scoops on *The Curse of the Cheese Pyramid* and *The Search for Sunken Treasure*. He has also received the Andersen 2000 Prize for Personality of the Year. One of his bestsellers won the 2002 eBook Award for world's best ratlings' electronic book. His works have been published all over the globe.

In his spare time, Mr. Stilton collects antique cheese rinds and plays golf. But what he most enjoys is telling stories to his nephew Benjamin.

THE RODENT'S GAZETTE

1. Main entrance
2. Printing presses (where the books and newspaper are printed)
3. Accounts department
4. Editorial room (where the editors, illustrators, and designers work)
5. Geronimo Stilton's office
6. Storage space for Geronimo's books

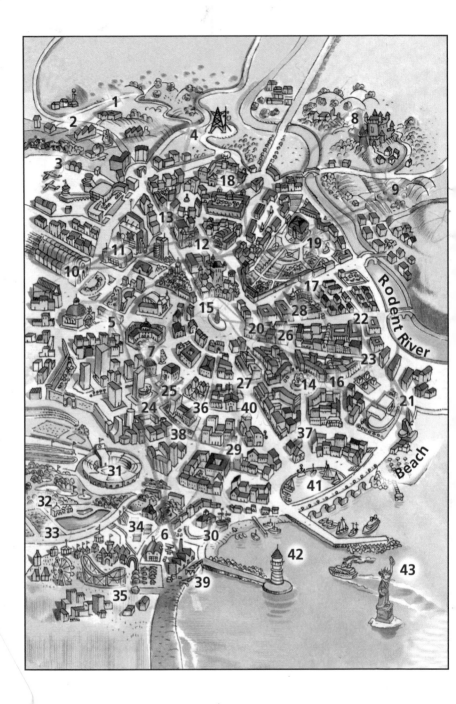

Map of New Mouse City

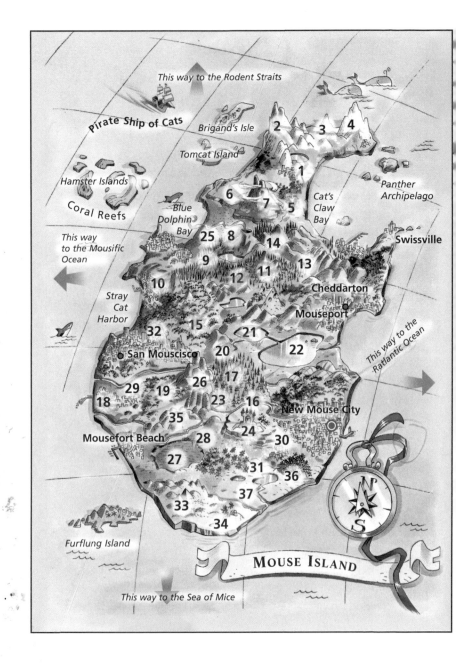

Map of Mouse Island

1. Big Ice Lake
2. Frozen Fur Peak
3. Slipperyslopes Glacier
4. Coldcreeps Peak
5. Ratzikistan
6. Transratania
7. Mount Vamp
8. Roastedrat Volcano
9. Brimstone Lake
10. Poopedcat Pass
11. Stinko Peak
12. Dark Forest
13. Vain Vampires Valley
14. Goose Bumps Gorge
15. The Shadow Line Pass
16. Penny Pincher Castle
17. Nature Reserve Park
18. Las Ratayas Marinas
19. Fossil Forest
20. Lake Lake
21. Lake Lakelake
22. Lake Lakelakelake
23. Cheddar Crag
24. Cannycat Castle
25. Valley of the Giant Sequoia
26. Cheddar Springs
27. Sulfurous Swamp
28. Old Reliable Geyser
29. Vole Vale
30. Ravingrat Ravine
31. Gnat Marshes
32. Munster Highlands
33. Mousehara Desert
34. Oasis of the Sweaty Camel
35. Cabbagehead Hill
36. Rattytrap Jungle
37. Rio Mosquito

Don't miss any of my other fabumouse adventures!

#1 Lost Treasure of the Emerald Eye

#2 The Curse of the Cheese Pyram

#3 Cat and Mouse in a Haunted House

#4 I'm Too Fond of My Fur!

#5 Four Mice Deep in the Jungle

#6 Paws Off, Cheddarface!

#7 Red Pizzas for a Blue Count

#8 Attack of the Bandit Cats

#9 A Fabumouse Vacation for Geronimo

#10 All Because o a Cup of Coffee

#11 It's Halloween, You 'Fraidy Mouse!

#12 Merry Christmas, Geronimo!

#13 The Phantom of the Subway

#14 The Temple o the Ruby of Fire

#15 The Mona Mousa Code

#16 A Cheese-Colored Camper

#17 Watch Your Whiskers, Stilton!

#18 Shipwreck on the Pirate Islands

#19 My Name Is Stilton, Geronimo Stilton

#20 Surf's Up, Geronimo!

#21 The Wild, Wild West

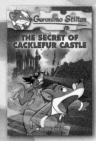

#22 The Secret of Cacklefur Castle

A Christmas Tale

#23 Valentine's Day Disaster

#24 Field Trip to Niagara Falls

#25 The Search for Sunken Treasure

#26 The Mummy with No Name

#27 The Christmas Toy Factory

#28 Wedding Crasher

and coming soon

#30 The Mouse Island Marathon

Dear mouse friends,
Thanks for reading, and farewell
till the next book.
It'll be another whisker-licking-good
adventure, and that's a promise!

Geronimo Stilton